Dear Parent:
Your child's love of reading starts here!

Every child learns to read in a different way and at his or her own speed. You can help your young reader improve and become more confident by encouraging his or her own interests and abilities. You can also guide your child's spiritual development by reading stories with biblical values and Bible stories, like I Can Read! books published by Zonderkidz. From books your child reads with you to the first books he or she reads alone, there are I Can Read! books for every stage of reading:

SHARED READING
Basic language, word repetition, and whimsical illustrations, ideal for sharing with your emergent reader.

BEGINNING READING
Short sentences, familiar words, and simple concepts for children eager to read on their own.

READING WITH HELP
Engaging stories, longer sentences, and language play for developing readers.

READING ALONE
Complex plots, challenging vocabulary, and high-interest topics for the independent reader.

ADVANCED READING
Short paragraphs, chapters, and exciting themes for the perfect bridge to chapter books.

I Can Read! books have introduced children to the joy of reading since 1957. Featuring award-winning authors and illustrators and a fabulous cast of beloved characters, I Can Read! books set the standard for beginning readers.

A lifetime of discovery begins with the magical words "I Can Read!"

Visit www.icanread.com for information on enriching your child's reading experience.
Visit www.zonderkidz.com for more Zonderkidz I Can Read! titles.

Suppose you are offering your gift at the altar. And you remember that your brother has something against you. Leave your gift in front of the altar. First go and make peace with your brother. Then come back and offer your gift.
—*Matthew 5:23–24*

zonder**kidz**.
The children's group
of Zondervan

www.zonderkidz.com

Mad Maddie Maxwell
ISBN-10: 0-310-71467-2
ISBN-13: 978-0-310-71467-5
Copyright © 2000, 2007 by Stacie K. B. Maslyn
Illustrations copyright © 2000 by Jane Schettle

Requests for information should be addressed to:
Zonderkidz, Grand Rapids, Michigan 49530

Library of Congress Cataloging-in-Publication Data

applied for

Art Direction: Jody Langley
Cover Design: Sarah Molegraaf

Printed in the United States of America

08 09 10 • 9 8 7 6 5 4 3 2

zonderkidz. **I Can Read!** BEGINNING 1 READING

Mad Maddie Maxwell

story by Stacie K.B. Maslyn
pictures by Jane Schettle

Maddie Joy Maxwell

ran from her room.

"Where is it?

Where is it?

My jump rope is missing."

Maddie yelled at her sister Julie.
"Julie, you took my jump rope
from under my bed!"

"Who, me?"

"Yes, you."

"Not me."

"Then who?"

"Seth."

Maddie ran past Julie.

"Get out of my way.

I can't stop to talk.

I can't stop to play.

My jump rope is missing.

Good-bye and good day!"

Maddie yelled at her brother Seth.
"Seth, you took my jump rope
from under my bed!"

"Who, me?"

"Yes, you."

"Not me."

"Then who?"

"Missy."

Maddie ran past Seth.

"Get out of my way.

I can't stop to talk.

I can't stop to play.

My jump rope is missing.

Good-bye and good day!"

Maddie thought of her big sister.

"It must be Missy.

She must have my jump rope.

Big sisters are like that."

She ran to find Missy.

Maddie did not wait to ask.
"Missy, you took my jump rope
from under my bed!"

"Who, me?"

"Yes, you."

"Not me."

"Then who?"

Missy smiled.

Missy stood up.

"Where are you going?"
Maddie yelled.

"Maybe you need to look
under your bed," said Missy.

Maddie folded her arms.

She put her nose in the air.

"It's dark and dusty under my bed.

You won't find it. Trust me!

You are wasting our time,"

Maddie said.

Missy pulled out a doll and a ball.

She pulled out a big mess

from under Maddie's bed.

"Where is it?" Maddie shouted.

"I gave you your chance!"

Missy pulled out her jump rope.

Then Maddie stopped yelling.

It was there all along.

It was in the mess under the bed.

She hung down her head.

Maddie felt bad.

"I have been so mean,"

Maddie said with a cry.

"I'm sorry, Missy.

No one will forgive me."

"I will forgive you," said Missy.

"And God will too.

Pray to him first

and then talk to the others."

Maddie said sorry,

and each one forgave her.

They played jump rope together.

Mad Maddie was happy that day.

VINCENT KIERNAN

Wikipedia: The Missing Manual